19.93

SandCastle 3

Homographs

Pete Presents the Presents

Carey Molter

ABDO
Publishing Company

Published by SandCastle™, an imprint of ABDO Publishing Company, 4940 Viking Drive, Edina, Minnesota 55435.

Cover and interior photo credits: Corel, Eyewire Images, Image 100, PhotoDisc, Stockbyte

Library of Congress Cataloging-in-Publication Data

Molter, Carey, 1973-
    Pete presents the presents / Carey Molter.
        p. cm. -- (Homographs)
    Includes index.
    Summary: Photographs and simple text introduce homophones, words with different meanings that are spelled the same but sound different.
    ISBN 1-57765-796-9
    1. English language--Homonyms--Juvenile literature. [1. English language--Homonyms.] I. Title.

PE1595 .M68 2002
428.1--dc21

                                                              2001053313

The SandCastle concept, content, and reading method have been reviewed and approved by a national advisory board including literacy specialists, librarians, elementary school teachers, early childhood education professionals, and parents.

Let Us Know

After reading the book, SandCastle would like you to tell us your stories about reading. What is your favorite page? Was there something hard that you needed help with? Share the ups and downs of learning to read. We want to hear from you! To get posted on the ABDO Publishing Company Web site, send us email at:

sandcastle@abdopub.com

About SandCastle™

Nonfiction books for the beginning reader

- Basic concepts of phonics are incorporated with integrated language methods of reading instruction. Most words are short, and phrases, letter sounds, and word sounds are repeated.

- Book levels are based on the ATOS™ for Books formula. Other considerations for readability include the number of words in each sentence, the number of characters in each word, and word lists based on curriculum frameworks.

- Full-color photography reinforces word meanings and concepts.

- "Words I Can Read" list at the end of each book teaches basic elements of grammar, helps the reader recognize the words in the text, and builds vocabulary.

- Reading levels are indicated by the number of flags on the castle.

SandCastle uses the following definitions for this series:

- Homographs: words that are spelled the same but sound different and have different meanings. *Easy memory tip: "-graph"= same look*

- Homonyms: words that are spelled and sound the same but have different meanings. *Easy memory tip: "-nym"= same name*

- Homophones: words that sound alike but are spelled differently and have different meanings. *Easy memory tip: "-phone"= sound alike*

Look for more SandCastle books in these three reading levels:

Level 1 (one flag)	**Level 2** (two flags)	**Level 3** (three flags)

Grades Pre-K to K 5 or fewer words per page	**Grades K to 1** 5 to 10 words per page	**Grades 1 to 2** 10 to 15 words per page

Note: Many of the pages in this book have fewer than 10 words due to the difficulty of the subject matter.

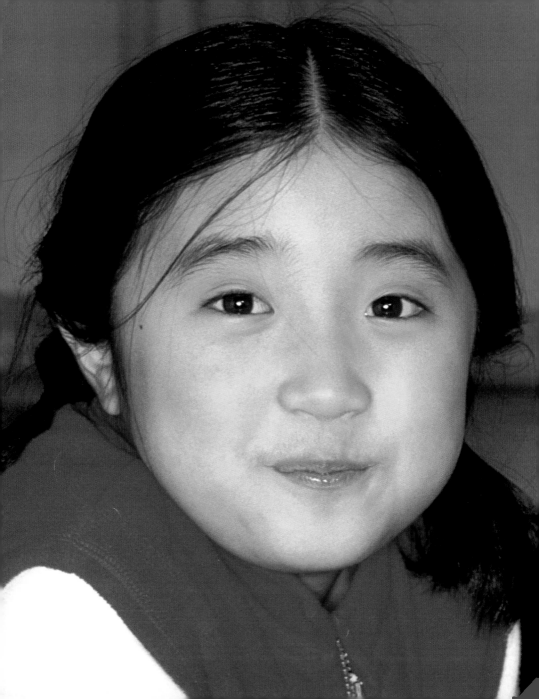

Homographs are words that are spelled the same but sound different and have different meanings.

Rosa got a present on her special day.

Her brother will present her birthday cake.

It is a carrot cake.

A minute is sixty seconds long.

We can time it with a stopwatch.

Stars seem minute from Earth.

Many are really very large.

The snack stand will close at six tonight.

These good friends put their heads close together.

We had fun on our trip to the desert.

Nina pretends to leave her friends.

She will not really desert them.

Farmers often use a combine to harvest hay.

Sara and Leo combine the cookie dough.

I refuse to go outside without a warm sweater.

The dump is a place for refuse.

The Lopez family computer
is in use.

My dad and I **use** spoons to eat our cereal.

Uncle Tom will wind up the kite string while I watch.

What does the kite need in order to fly?

(wind)

Words I Can Read

Nouns

A noun is a person, place, or thing

birthday (BURTH-day)
  p. 7
brother (BRUHTH-ur)
  p. 7
carrot (KAR-uht) p. 7
cake (KAYK) p. 7
cereal (SIHR-ee-uhl)
  p. 19
combine (KOM-bine)
  p. 14
computer
  (kuhm-PYOO-tur)
  p. 18
cookie (KUK-ee) p. 15
dad (DAD) p. 19
day (DAY) p. 6
desert (DEZ-urt) p. 12
dough (DOH) p. 15
dump (DUHMP) p. 17

family (FAM-uh-lee)
  p. 18
farmers (FARM-urz)
  p. 14
friends (FRENDZ)
  pp. 11, 13
fun (FUHN) p. 12
hay (HAY) p. 14
heads (HEDZ) p. 11
homographs
  (HOM-uh-grafss) p. 5
kite (KITE) pp. 20, 21
meanings (MEE-ningz)
  p. 5
minute (MIN-it) p. 8
order (OR-dur) p. 21
place (PLAYSS) p. 17
present (PREZ-uhnt)
  p. 6

refuse (REF-yooss)
  p. 17
seconds (SEK-uhndz)
  p. 8
six (SIKS) p. 10
snack (SNAK) p. 10
spoons (SPOONZ)
  p. 19
stand (STAND) p. 10
stars (STARZ) p. 9
stopwatch
  (STOP-wahch) p. 8
string (STRING) p. 20
sweater (SWET-ur)
  p. 16
trip (TRIP) p. 12
use (YOOSS) p. 18
wind (WIND) p. 21
words (WURDZ) p. 5

Proper Nouns

A proper noun is the name of a person, place, or thing

Earth (URTH) p. 9
Leo (LEE-oh) p. 15
Lopez (LOH-pez) p. 18

Nina (NEE-nuh) p. 13
Rosa (RO-zuh) p. 6
Sara (SAIR-uh) p. 15

Uncle Tom
  (UHNG-kuhl TOM)
  p. 20

Pronouns

A pronoun is a word that replaces a noun

I (EYE) pp. 16, 19, 20

it (IT) pp. 7, 8

many (MEN-ee) p. 9

she (SHEE) p. 13

them (THEM) p. 13

we (WEE) pp. 8, 12

what (WUHT) p. 21

Verbs

A verb is an action or being word

are (AR) pp. 5, 9

can (KAN) p. 8

close (KLOHZ) p. 10

combine (kuhm-BINE)
p. 15

desert (di-ZURT) p. 13

does (DUHZ) p. 21

eat (EET) p. 19

fly (FLYE) p. 21

go (GOH) p. 16

got (GOT) p. 6

had (HAD) p. 12

harvest (HAR-vist) p. 14

have (HAV) p. 5

is (IZ) pp. 7, 8, 17, 18

leave (LEEV) p. 13

need (NEED) p. 21

present (pri-ZENT) p. 7

pretends
(pree-TENDZ) p. 13

put (PUT) p. 11

refuse (ri-FYOOZ) p. 16

seem (SEEM) p. 9

sound (SOUND) p. 5

spelled (SPELD) p. 5

time (TIME) p. 8

use (YOOZ) pp. 14, 19

watch (WOCH) p. 20

will (WIL)
pp. 7, 10, 13, 20

wind (WINDE) p. 20

Adjectives

An adjective describes something

different (DIF-ur-uhnt)
p. 5

good (GUD) p. 11

her (HUR) pp. 6, 7, 13

large (LARJ) p. 9

long (LAWNG) p. 8

minute (mye-NOOT)
p. 9

my (MYE) p. 19

our (OUR) pp. 12, 19

sixty (SIKS-tee) p. 8

special (SPESH-uhl)
p. 6

their (THAIR) p. 11

these (THEEZ) p. 11

warm (WORM) p. 16

23

Adverbs

An adverb tells how, when, or where something happens

close (KLOHSS) p. 11

often (OF-uhn) p. 14

outside (out-SIDE)
  p. 16

really (REE-lee)
  pp. 9, 13

same (SAYM) p. 5

together
  (tuh-GETH-ur) p. 11

tonight (tuh-NITE)
  p. 10

up (UHP) p. 20

very (VER-ee) p. 9